This Faber book belongs to

....

NUTRIENTS

SETLIST

SUN
LIGHT

**For the peas in my pod –
Sean, Teddy and Bobo.
C. F.**

**For Casper. You are
bonkers, and I wouldn't
want it any other way.
A. M.**

BUTTER
NUTTY
SQUASH

FUN
FUN
FUN

FESTIVAL

First published in the UK in 2020, by
Faber and Faber Limited, Bloomsbury House,
74–77 Great Russell Street, London WC1B 3DA.
Text copyright © Clare Foges, 2020. Illustration copyright ©
Al Murphy, 2020. ISBN 978-0-571-35286-9 All rights reserved.
Printed in India
1 3 5 7 9 10 8 6 4 2
The moral rights of Clare Foges and Al Murphy have been
asserted. A CIP record for this book is available
from the British Library.

AIR

FABER & FABER

has published children's books
since 1929. Some of our very first
publications included *Old Possum's
Book of Practical Cats* by T. S. Eliot,
starring the now world-famous
Macavity, and *The Iron Man* by
Ted Hughes. Our catalogue at the
time said that 'it is by reading
such books that children learn the
difference between the shoddy and
the genuine'. We still believe in
the power of reading to transform
children's lives.

ACCESS
ALL
AREAS

VEGSTOCK

*ACTUALLY
A FRUIT

WATER

↠ A FABER PICTURE BOOK ↞

VEG PATCH PARTY

CLARE FOGES & AL MURPHY

Every night down on the Farm
When Farmer stops for tea,

When all the cows are tucked up tight
And all the pigs asleep...

The vegetables start waking up.
They stretch and rise and shine.

They drag out lots of stages
Cos it's VEGGIE PARTY TIME!

POTATO is the first on stage
With backing band The Chips.
He shouts 'VEGGIES, ARE YOU READDDY!'
Then plays his latest hits.

She gets the parsnips jivin'
And she sets the turnips jumpin'.

SO conga like a carrot,
Party like a pea,
Rock out like a radish, **YEAH!**
And boogie like a bean!

It's called the veg patch party.
It's muddy, loud and fun...
So get your veggie wiggle on
And rock out **EVERYONE!**

Now...
RED HOT CHILLIS
take the stage –
The coolest band you've seen.
They play their rockin' music
To a crowd of runner beans.

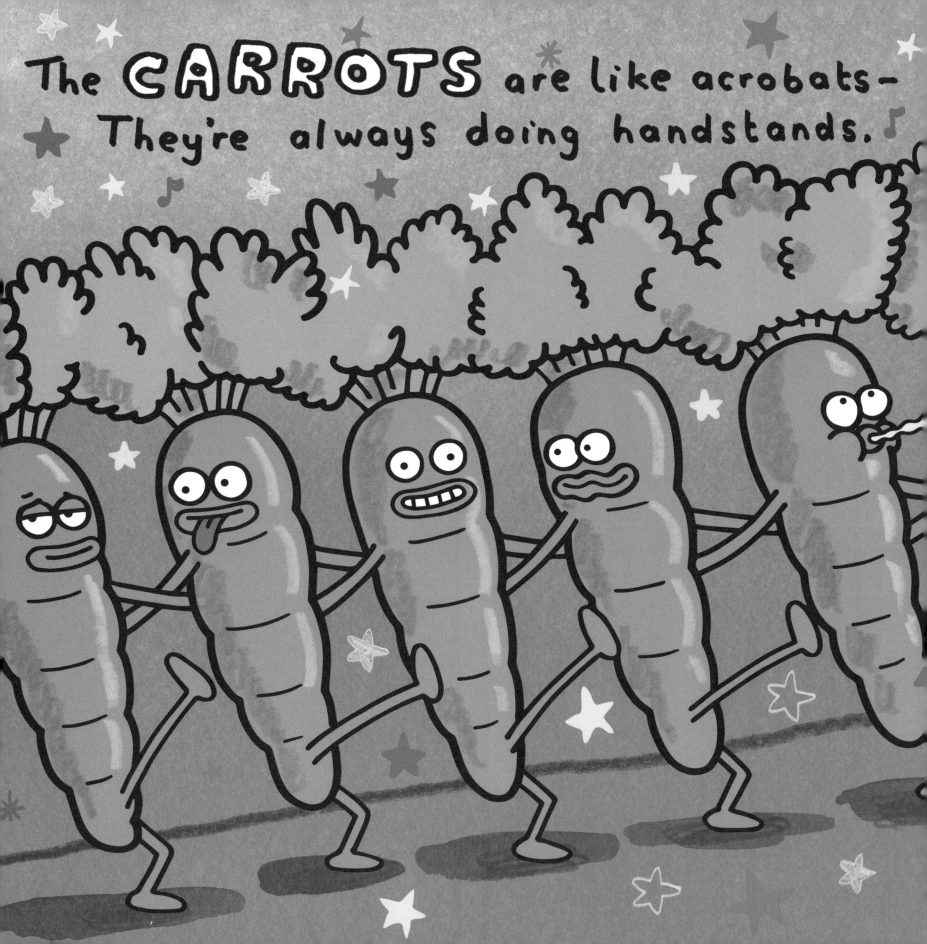

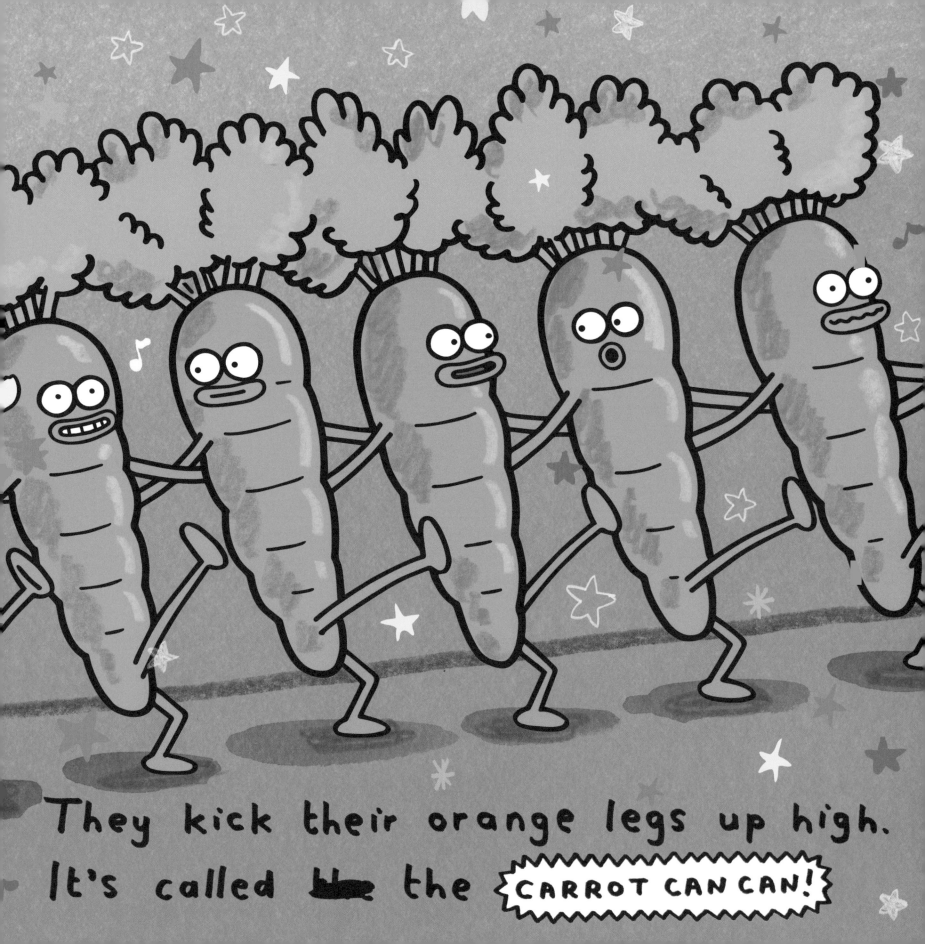

They kick their orange legs up high.
It's called ~~is~~ the **CARROT CAN CAN!**

The **PEAS** get so excited.
They bounce and scream and shout.
Up next on stage it's Techno King-
Yes...

SO conga like a carrot,
Party like a pea,
Rock out like a radish, **YEAH!**
And boogie like a bean!

It's called the veg patch party.
It's muddy, loud and fun...
So get your veggie wiggle on
And rock out EVERYONE!

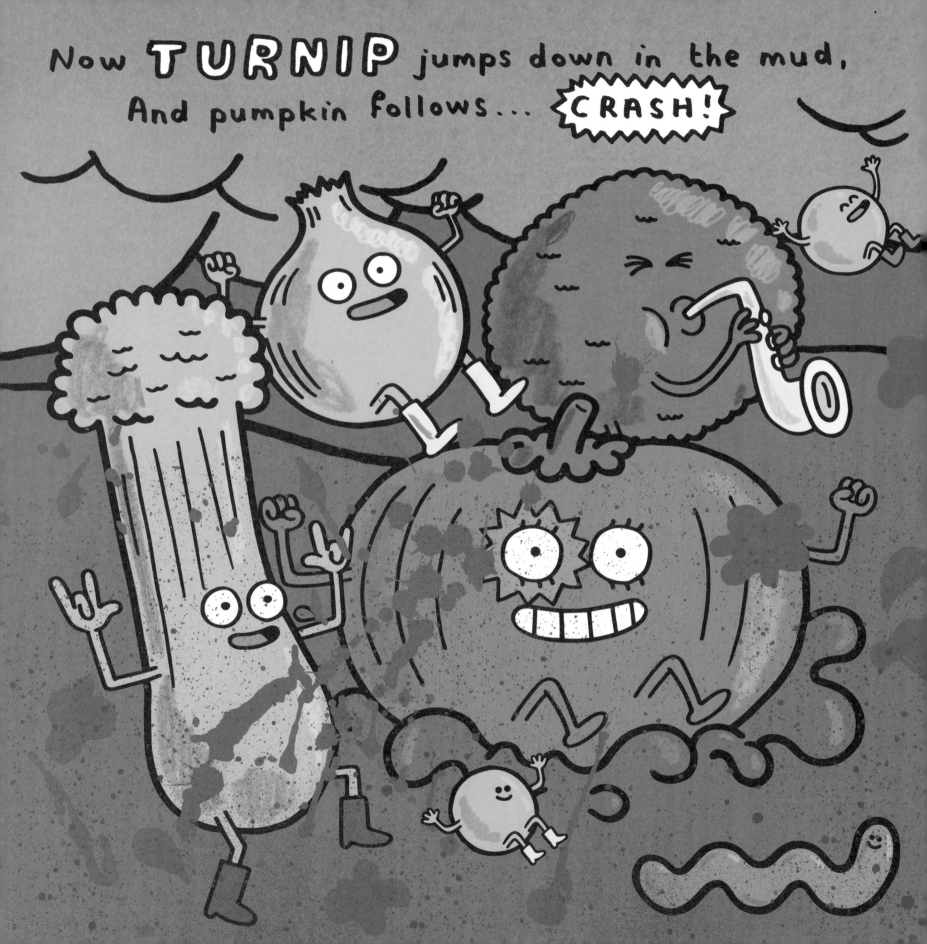

Next the peas all tumble in.
They skid, they skate, they {SPLASH!}

Check out those veggies going mad.
They're all on stage together!

SO conga like a carrot,
Party like a pea,
Rock out like a radish, **YEAH!**
And boogie like a bean!

It's called the veg patch party.
It's muddy, loud and fun...
So get your veggie wiggle on
And rock out EVERYONE!

YES...

So now you know what happens
When the moon is shining white
The veggies have a crazy time
And party through the night!

So conga like a carrot...